The Puffin Keeper

AEL

RGO

The Puffin Keeper

Illustrated by

Benji Davies

PUFFIN
an imprint of Penguin Random House Canada Young Readers,
a division of Penguin Random House of Canada Limited

Originally published in the UK by Puffin Books, 2020
Published in hardcover by Puffin Canada, 2022

1 2 3 4 5 6 7 8 9 10

Printed in China

Library and Archives Canada Cataloguing in Publication

Title: The puffin keeper / Michael Morpurgo ; illustrated by Benji Davies.
Names: Morpurgo, Michael, author. | Davies, Benji, illustrator.
Description: Originally published: London : Puffin, 2020.
Identifiers: Canadiana (print) 20210207736 | Canadiana (ebook) 20210207744 |
ISBN 9780735271807 (hardcover) | ISBN 9780735271814 (EPUB)
Classification: LCC PZ7.M825 Pu 2022 | DDC j823/.914—dc23

Library of Congress Control Number: 2021937985

www.penguinrandomhouse.ca

Penguin
Random House
PUFFIN CANADA

To the three Lane girls, Clare, Christine, and Anna.
Daughters of the Puffin man — M.M.

For all the members of my family who lived through
and were lucky enough to survive the times
in which this book is set — I salute you — B.D.

Chapter One

It was Benjamin Postlethwaite's job all his long life to make sure the light shone brightly high up in the lighthouse on Puffin Island where he lived. Not once in all his years as the lighthouse keeper had he ever let his light go out. All the sailors and seafarers that sailed or steamed past the lighthouse in the fog would hear his foghorn sounding, see his light guiding them through, and be grateful for it. Without Benjamin Postlethwaite many a ship would have come too close to the shore around Scilly, and been driven on to the rocks, and many a sailor would have been drowned. But sometimes even the brightest light on a lighthouse cannot save a ship.

One stormy night, a four-masted schooner —
Pelican she was called — sailing from New York
and bound for Liverpool, with thirty passengers
and crew on board, was driven by angry seas
on to the rocks just off the Scilly Isles in the
Western Approaches.

The sails were soon in tatters, three of her masts broken. She was helpless in the towering waves, and was sinking fast.

From high in his lighthouse, Benjamin Postlethwaite saw it all. He heard her timbers grinding and groaning as she settled on the rocks, heard the cries of the people on board. He knew at once what he had to do.

That night Benjamin Postlethwaite saved thirty lives, men, women and children — my own mother was one of them. And I was one of those children. Allen Williams. Five years old I was. Somehow, and I don't remember how, just before the ship sank, we were all able to clamber down, or jump over on to one of the rocks, where we found ourselves stranded, still at some distance from the shore, with barely room to stand, and at the mercy of huge waves crashing around us, every one of them threatening to wash us away. All Mother and I could do was cling to one another, and hope.

Then, when all hope seemed lost, we saw through the darkness a boat coming for us — one man in a tiny rowing boat that was riding mountainous seas.

Benjamin Postlethwaite rowed out to our rescue that night, back and forth five times from the shore, through the surging surf in his little boat, and brought us all safe to the island.

In the warmth of his lighthouse, wrapped in blankets, he gave us hot sweet tea and cookies, and we sat out the raging storm around his fire, rubbed one another down and warmed ourselves through, each of us astonished at his bravery and his calm. Every one of us must have thanked him a dozen times from the bottom of our hearts.

He hardly said a word to anyone in reply, scarcely even looked at us. We owed our lives to this silent unsmiling man. I sat watching him, as he made pot after pot of tea, as he attended to our every need, did all he could to make us comfortable and warm.

I caught his eye just once, and smiled. He smiled back and that was the only time I saw him smile.

All around the walls of the lighthouse, I noticed, there were dozens of paintings, all of them of boats: little boats, big boats, steam boats, sailing boats, out at sea, in storm or calm, leaving harbor, coming into harbor. Most were quite small, and most painted on bits of wood or cardboard. There were drawings scattered everywhere, on tables, on the floor, on shelves. All these paintings and drawings were simply signed, BEN, at the top right-hand corner in big letters.

One of the pictures I especially loved. It was a small picture painted on a fragment of wood, of a four-masted schooner just like ours sailing through the waves past a lighthouse. He must have seen me looking at it, I think, because just before we were all taken off his island by the lifeboat the next day, he came up to me on the quayside and gave it to me. Before I had got over the surprise, before I had time to thank him, he had walked away and was climbing the rocky steps up to his lighthouse.

That was the last I saw of Benjamin Postlethwaite or of Puffin Island for a very long time. But I never forgot him, nor how he had saved my life, and Mother's life, and the lives of

all the others too. Wherever I went in my life after that I took his picture with me, if I could. The memories of that day and what he did for us were to stay with me all my life.

Chapter Two

Mother and I were only on board the *Pelican* that night because, just after I was born, Father had fallen off his horse in Central Park, in New York, and died. We were on our way five years later from New York to live with Grandfather and Grandmother in England, on Dartmoor in Devon. They were Father's family. Mother had nowhere else to go, no one else to turn to. I had never met them. They were cold gray people, living in a cold gray house, on a cold gray moor, where I spent most of my time with a cold gray nanny in the nursery upstairs.

Mother was not well for much of the time, so there were many weeks when she stayed in her bedroom and I was not allowed to see her. The doctor came to visit her often. I asked how she was, and all he would say was that she was "fragile." I never really knew what that meant. I only knew she was so sad in her heart that she hardly spoke, because Father had died. I was sad too, but not for Father. I had no memory of him. But I was sad because Mother was sad.

Miss Duval (Miss Devil, to me, under my breath) was my nanny to begin with, then also my governess and my persecutor, and she ruled my life. She ruled with her ruler too. Her favorite punishment, for dirty fingernails, untidy hair, for hiding rice pudding under my spoon so I didn't have to eat it, was to make me hold out my hand, and then she'd hit me with the edge of her ruler on my knuckles.

I lived in dread of her ruler.

Worse still, she wouldn't let me have my precious picture on the wall because it was not in a frame like a proper picture, and anyway, she said, it looked as if it had been painted by a child, and that it wasn't worth hanging. So I kept it hidden secretly under a loose floorboard and took it out whenever I could, to remember, to imagine myself there again in the lighthouse with Benjamin Postlethwaite.

There were a lot of rules, Grandfather's rules. I was never allowed to go up the front stairs, nor run in the house, never to speak until I was spoken to, and never to talk at meals. I had to have a cold bath every morning, because Grandfather said I would not grow up strong and be a proper man unless I did.

I lived in terror of Grandfather. But Grandmother was never nasty to me, mostly just somber and silent, sitting by the window at her embroidery, at the beck and call of Grandfather. I think she hardly noticed I was there. She was nasty about Mother sometimes, though, they both were, and would call her "that French woman," when they thought I wasn't listening. I think even as a child I knew that somehow they blamed her for what had happened to Father, who had been their only son.

Mother hated living in that house as much I did, but I knew she had nowhere else to go. When she was feeling better, she would slip softly into my room at night, sit on my bed and read to me; and we would often talk long into the early hours about Father and New York, and about the night the *Pelican* foundered on the rocks, and about Benjamin Postlethwaite, and his lighthouse, and his pictures. I would lift up the floorboard and show Mother the picture under the light of her lamp. With the flame flickering on it, the ship seemed to be moving through the waves, and clouds scudding across the skies. Just to look at the picture under that lamplight made me feel as if we were there again in the lighthouse with all the other survivors shivering away our cold in front of Benjamin Postlethwaite's fire.

It was one night as we were looking at the picture again that Mother suggested that maybe I should write to Benjamin Postlethwaite to thank him for my picture. It would be good for me anyway, she said, to practice my writing. So I wrote him a letter, thanking him for saving Mother and me and the others, and telling him how much I loved his picture and how one day I would come back to see him on his island, in his lighthouse. Mother addressed the envelope, and I was with her when she posted the letter in the mailbox at the end of the lane. For weeks, for months, I waited every morning for a reply. He never wrote back.

THE PUFFIN KEEPER

Then I had some happy news, which was also sad news at the same time. Miss Duval, or rather Miss Devil, who was in one her great rages with me, announced to us all at breakfast one morning that she was going to leave, because I was "impossible," she said. This, I have always thought, was because I had called her Miss Devil to her face the night before, by mistake, and I had refused to apologize. Her announcement came as a wonderful surprise to me. Happy news indeed.

But later that same day, after Miss Devil had gone, Grandfather called me into his study. Mother and Grandmother were there, and I could see Mother had been crying. He told me that since I was eight years old now, and Miss Duval had left — which was my fault, he said — he had decided it was time for me to be sent away to boarding school, that it was about time

I learned to grow up and stand on my own two feet, that it would be good for me, make me a proper man. This was the sad news, the most dreadful news. I turned to Mother, and begged her not to let him make me go. But Mother was in tears by now, and ran crying from the room.

Chapter Three

How I missed her at that boarding school, especially in my first years away, but I loved her letters. I kept them all in my tuck box in the basement of the school. And I kept my picture there too. I would sit for hours sometimes down there, reading her letters, and looking at my picture. I ran away twice, but each time I was caught and brought back to my prison of a school.

The headmaster, Mr. Mortimer, was furious with me. The more enraged he became, the more his bushy eyebrows waggled, and the more I felt like laughing out loud. He couldn't scare me, not after Grandfather. "If you want to run away, boy," he thundered, "then for your punishment, when all the other boys have their breaktime after lunch, you will go on a cross-country run. Every day for the next two months, whatever the weather. See how you like that!"

As it turned out I did like that. I liked the running. I liked being alone. I loved the rain and the wind and the mud, and the birds I'd see down by the river, the herons, the kingfishers, the cormorants. In fact, I became so good at

cross-country running that after a while I was chosen to run for the school team. I won races and medals, and everyone seemed to like that, Mr. Mortimer most all. Now he waggled his eyebrows at me in open admiration and appreciation.

Then one day in my art class with Mr. Carter — the only teacher in the school I liked and respected — I discovered I could draw and

I could paint, and that I liked it. After that I painted ships a lot, and lighthouses of course. I found myself copying Benjamin Postlethwaite's painting. I never had it in front of me. It stayed hidden and safe in my tuck box. But I didn't need it. I knew it by heart, every wave, every gull and gannet riding the wind, every brushstroke.

Mr. Carter told me often how much he liked my ships and lighthouses, but that maybe I should try to widen my scope, paint more fruit and flowers, birds and bees, landscapes and portraits. I tried, but ships and lighthouses were always my favorite subjects.

It was about this time that I read *Robinson Crusoe* for the first time. I read it again and again. After that I loved to lose myself in books, but they too were mostly about islands or lighthouses or ships — *Treasure Island, The Coral Island* and *Moby Dick*. The library became my favorite place of refuge in this noisy, boisterous place. I was a bit of a loner, not because I wanted to be. I was just like that. Books became friends to me. To finish a book I would read late into the night, sometimes with a flashlight under my blankets, which was against the school rules. I was caught often. And that meant more of

Mr. Mortimer's waggling eyebrows, and more cross-country runs. That was fine by me. Life was getting better all the time.

Then, joy of joys, Mother wrote me a letter telling me she had decided she had had enough of the gray stone house on the moor, had enough of living there, that she was missing me and wanted to be near me. She was coming to live near the school during my last two years there. She had found a job. She was to become the French teacher at my school. I could not have been happier.

So the next term and for the rest of my two years at school, I lived with Mother in her cottage in the village nearby. I had a proper home again. I went for long walks with her at weekends, talked often of Benjamin Postlethwaite and his paintings. She was always there watching me now when I was winning my races. She would call out loud so that everyone could hear. "Bravo, Allen! *Allez! Félicitations!*" And everyone loved her Frenchness. Me too.

Chapter Four

So my schooldays passed, much more happily now. Holidays came and went.

And then one day during my last term at school, I found myself in the library, searching for yet another book, and I happened by pure chance to come across an old magazine on the table. There were always lots of old magazines lying about, most of them called *The Illustrated London News*. I loved looking at the photographs in them, pictures of how it was in years gone by.

This particular magazine was dated 1926. I have no idea why I opened it. I just did. Looking up at me from the magazine was a photo of the still unsmiling face of Benjamin Postlethwaite. I thought at first I must have been imagining things. I wasn't. Behind him was his lighthouse, and beside this picture there was another, of the wreck of the *Pelican*.

The headline read: LIGHTHOUSE KEEPER HERO REFUSES MEDAL. And there it was, the whole story of the miraculous rescue, as told by many of our fellow survivors from the wreck of the *Pelican*. According to the article, it was too rough for the boat to come alongside Puffin Island, and Benjamin Postlethwaite had stood up there on the quay shouting everything down to the reporter who had asked him why he had refused to accept the medal for such a courageous act.

The Wreck of The Pelican

Lighthouse Keeper

HER

Benjamin Postlethwaite, aged 53, the lighthouse keeper of Puffin Island, has refused to accept a medal for saving the lives of thirty men, and children.

Ref:

M

"I'm not saying nothing, excepting to say it were done because it were needed to be done. There were lives needed saving. And there's an end to it. Life isn't about medals and that. They can keep their medals. Now off you go, and leave me be. I got my lighthouse to look after." And he just turned and walked away.

There was another photograph of him walking away up the rocky steps to his lighthouse, just how I remembered he had on that day twelve years before, just after he had given me his picture.

It was seeing that magazine, that photograph of him walking away up the steps, that gave me the idea. The same day I wrote a letter to Benjamin Postlethwaite, addressed to the lighthouse on Puffin Island, asking if he would mind if I came to visit him one day. I wrote the address on the envelope, but I also painted a picture around the address — it was a copy of his picture — hoping he would remember who I was when he saw the envelope.

I never received a reply. Mother wrote too. She was sure the address was right. *The Lighthouse. Puffin Island. Scilly Isles. Cornwall.* We heard nothing. Mother said that maybe he was no longer the lighthouse keeper and had left the island, or that he had died. She also said that maybe he just wanted to be left alone.

But I could not stop thinking about him. I had to find out for myself what had happened to him. I made up my mind that when I finally left school, the first thing I had to do would be to go back to Puffin Island to find the man who had saved our lives and thank him, and thank him for his picture too.

I told Mother that I was going on a journey of exploration. She had often told me how I should one day have to explore the world for myself, to discover who I was, what I wanted to be. So she was happy enough for me to go. I told her that I'd be back in a month or so, but I didn't tell her where I was going in case she wanted to come with me. This was to be my adventure, mine alone.

I took the train down to Penzance, and then the steamer across to the islands, the picture in my suitcase. I asked after Benjamin Postlethwaite at the post office, and was told he was still living on his own out on Puffin Island. "But folk don't go there," I was told. "And these days he don't come here more than once or twice a year. Keeps himself to himself. Pity about the lighthouse. Old Ben, he lived

for that lighthouse, you know." I asked what had happened to the lighthouse. "They shut it down, a year ago now. Don't you know? It weren't needed no more, not these days, that's what they told him. Saving money don't save lives, that's what I think. Not easy when they tell you you're not needed."

I found a boatman to take me over to the island. It was a choppy crossing that churned my stomach. I was feeling ill almost at once. The boatman was full of cheerful banter. "You get some storms out here," he told me, rather enjoying my discomfort, I thought. I felt like telling him I knew about storms around the lighthouse, that I'd lived through one, but only just, thanks to Benjamin Postlethwaite. "You haven't come to see the puffins, have you?" He went on. "Hope not, cos there ain't

none. Haven't been no puffins on Puffin Island
for a hundred years or more. Only old Ben
lives on Puffin Island. And he won't welcome
you neither. Don't say too much. Grumpy old
so-and-so, he is."

I was only half listening to his prattling. I
was determined not to give him the satisfaction
of being sick. I tried to concentrate on the
gannets and the terns diving into the sea,
and the seal lying out on a black rock, maybe
the very rock I had stood on with Mother and
all the others twelve years before, as we saw
Benjamin Postlethwaite coming to rescue us in
his little boat.

And there was the sight of the towering
lighthouse looming ever closer, ever higher,
and I hadn't been sick. That made me feel a lot
better. We were nearly there.

Chapter Five

Left on the quayside, watching the boat leaving and then ploughing her way through the waves, I wondered for a moment how I was going to get back. I hadn't even thought of that. I climbed the rocky steps up from the quay to the door of the lighthouse, took a deep breath and knocked.

The door opened almost at once. And there he was. Older, more raggedy, straggling hair the same. "I seen you coming," he said. "You're the boy, in't you? That one off the *Pelican*. I been expecting you." He turned and led me up the steps. "Come along up. And shut the door behind you. That wind don't never stop blowing."

He sat me down by the fire and brought me a cup of sweet tea, just as he had twelve years before. "Strange you coming today. You'm the second visitor. Visitors don't come over much, hardly at all. That's the way I like it." I was only half listening to him. I was too distracted. Every inch of the wall was hidden by paintings. And, just as I remembered, there were drawings scattered everywhere. "You still got my painting?"

I nodded, lost for words. I opened my suitcase, took it out and showed him. He smiled. "It was a good one. I do good ones sometimes. You seen yourself, have you?"

He was pointing to the wall above the fireplace. I hadn't noticed it until then, a page

of photos from a newspaper. "You're the one in the middle. See? They're all there, everyone I took off the *Pelican* that day. That's you, in't it? You've growed a fair bit. Someone sent me the newspaper. I cut it out, so's I'd always remember. Not a night to forget. You want to meet my other visitor? Blew in, he did, this morning early. Lost himself, I reckon. Cold he was. Hurt hisself too, his leg."

He was looking down at a cardboard box near the fire — for sticks, I thought. I was wrong. The old man bent down, reached in, and held up a puffin. I had only ever seen puffins in picture books before. He was brighter colored than I had ever imagined, and smaller, too small for its head and its outsized beak. He did not struggle, just seemed rather bemused as he gazed about the room.

"He's only young," said Benjamin Postlethwaite. "He must have flown into the glass at the top of the lighthouse, the lantern room. No light in there any more to warn him away. More's the pity. Just glass. Can't see glass. Hurt his leg, poor soul. I'll make him right,

you'll see. He'll need a splint for that leg, and it'll need time to heal. We'll go out in the boat and find him fish. He likes sand eels. All puffins like sand eels. It's just about all they eat, y'know. And we got to make this one strong again. We got a leg to mend and a life to save. So you've come at just the right time. You can give me a hand with the fishing. Will you do that?"

I could hardly say no. I didn't want to say no. So I stayed. I found myself sleeping on a lumpy old mattress on the floor that night, in front of the fire, with his paintings all around, and with the puffin beside me in a cage I helped to make. I lived on a diet of porridge and fish. The porridge tasted of fish and the fish tasted of porridge. But after a day out at sea fishing I would have been happy eating anything. Finding enough sand eels was never easy, but I think our little puffin knew he had to eat to live.

We both adored him, sitting over him, feeding him and cooing him back to life and strength.

However loud the storms raged outside, however much the lighthouse shook, that little bird became the center of our world. Only look at him and we had to smile. Nothing mattered more to us than to see him fly. And as the days passed his strength grew, and his leg mended — he'd walk with a bit of limp, but he could walk well enough. Soon we could see his wings were longing to fly, and we knew the time for his release would be coming. But first we let him out of his cage so he could try out his wings in the safety of the room.

He flew more like a moth, his wings beating fast and furious, and when he landed, he landed clumsily, often toppling over before regaining his balance and his composure. And always after these experimental flights around the room he would look at us quizzically, as if to say: "I've proved it. I can fly, which is more than you can. Now set me free, let me go." That puffin spoke with his eyes, and I understood. I understood, but I did not want to let him go. Neither, I could tell, did the old man. We put it off as long as we could, dreading being without him.

When the day for his release came, we fed him his sand eels for the last time, climbed together to the lantern room at the top of the lighthouse, and opened the window. Ben took the puffin out of his cage, and handed him to me, tears in his eyes. "I can't," he said. "You do it." And so in two hands I held our puffin out of the window, felt his beating heart, opened my hands and off he flew.

But he did not fly away. Instead he circled the lighthouse again and again, almost as if he was as reluctant to leave as we were to release him, before flying off, down to the sea, skimming the waves.

Then he came back over the far end of the island, exploring, I thought, loving his flying again, then soaring away and away until he was gone.

That same evening, I was sitting deep in my thoughts, thoughts of the friend we had just lost, when Ben said. "He'll be back, you'll see. Not the last we've seen of that fellow. And when the time comes for you to go, you'll be back as well. That's what I think. But I don't want you to go, not just yet. I want to show you something." He fetched down a shoebox from a shelf. "Have a look in there," he said. I opened it. It was full of letters. I took one out. It was one of the letters I had written to him, with a painted envelope. It turned out that all the letters in the box were the ones I had written to him, and there was the one from Mother too. Not one of them had been opened. He told me why.

"I can't read," he said. "Never had no schooling. Course, I knew they came from you, because of the ship picture on the envelope. But I couldn't read them."

"I can read," I said. I didn't think about it before I was saying it. "I can stay and teach you, if you like."

The Lighthouse
Puffin Island
Scilly Isles
CORNWALL

Chapter Six

So that's what happened. I stayed with him in the lighthouse and over the next couple of months, I taught him to read. He learned fast because he wanted to learn. He didn't want me to read the letters, he said. He wanted to read them himself. And so he did, in time. He read them out aloud to me over and over again. We read from magazines. We read *Robinson Crusoe*. We went to the library on St. Mary's, across the water, and I found him the books I loved. I read them to him. He loved *Treasure Island* especially. He read it to me again and again.

We lived in a world apart on Puffin Island. We knew that well enough from our visits to the library, or to fetch in supplies. It was in town on St. Mary's one day that we found out about the threat of war. It was all anyone was talking about. We didn't pay it much attention. Back in the lighthouse we never talked about it. It was too troubling, part of a world we were very

happy not to know, not to be part of.

Ben painted every evening, and
I painted with
him. I basked
in his approval
of my efforts.
That was how
he taught, never
with instruction
or advice, simply
with a nod, or a smile
of appreciation.

We talked, we fished, we
read, we painted. We became
the best of friends. But Ben had
sad days, sad times, dark times,
when the smile left him, and a
somber silence descended on the

lighthouse. I knew then he must be thinking of our puffin, missing him as I was. Or maybe he was thinking of his lighthouse, how the light had gone out, never to be lit again, how he was no longer needed. Only the reading, the stories, helped bring him out of himself and cheered him.

And then one day, a wonderful and most unexpected thing happened. We were out in the boat fishing, when we saw a puffin circling the lighthouse. Around and around it he flew, then came floating down towards us. "It's him!" said Ben. He had no doubt about it. "That's him right enough," he said. "No other puffin like him. It's our puffin, got to be!"

The puffin was waiting for us on the quay. He was walking up and down, and limping. He was our puffin all right. "I told you he would come back," Ben said. "We were friends. Good friends never forget." He smiled a lot more these days.

Our puffin came back again and again after
that first time, and that always lifted his spirits.
And sometimes now our puffin was not alone.

There might be one or two others with him, and once I counted ten of them circling the lighthouse, then flying out to the far end of the island, landing there, making it their own. I had never seen Ben so happy. And for me too it was a moment of sheer joy that I shall never forget.

I knew Mother would be worrying by now where I was and why I had been so long away. So I sent her a letter and one of my paintings. After that there were weekly letters from her begging me to come home. I sent her more paintings, and told her all about Ben and our life on the island, and about the puffins, and that I'd be home soon. But I did not want to leave. I had found my home on this rugged island with my hermit painter friend. I never wanted to leave. But I didn't tell Mother that.

A supply boat came out once every month or so. The boatman was always talkative, too talkative. We'd see him coming from far away, and Ben would stay inside and hide away. So I was on my own on the quay one morning when the boatman arrived. He was waving a telegram at me. I opened it at once. It was from

Mother, telling me my call-up papers had come, that I had to go home.

Chapter Seven

I had no choice. I had to go to join up. I left on the steamer that same afternoon. All Ben said as we said goodbye on the quayside was: "You be sure to come back. I'll be waiting. Puffins'll be waiting." And he walked away, bowed with sadness, not looking back. It wasn't until we were out of sight of Scilly that I remembered I had left my picture behind. I remember thinking that at least it was where it belonged if I didn't come back. It belonged with Ben in the lighthouse on Puffin Island.

MICHAEL MORPURGO

I did see Mother once before I went to join up. She was in tears much of the time, about the invasion of her beloved France. The Germans were in Paris, occupying, marching through the streets. It was all she could think of. All too soon I found myself in uniform. I joined the navy, because I loved the sea, and because I thought that I'd rather drown than be blown to pieces.

I didn't like the war, but I liked being a sailor. My shipmates were a good lot, most of them, and I made good friends. But a year or so later my ship, HMS *Avenger*, an aircraft carrier, was torpedoed in the Mediterranean Sea off the coast of North Africa. Six hundred of us died, including my best friend, John. I was one of only thirty-five survivors. But this time I was not picked up and saved by a lighthouse keeper, but by German sailors from a German ship. I spent

74

the rest of the war in a prison camp in Poland. I escaped from it — I'd never liked being shut in — and ran away just as I had run away from school, ran fast, but not fast enough.

I was caught a few days later. Punishment was a month in solitary confinement. I would have preferred being sent on a cross-country run. But it gave me time to think, to plan what to do when I got out of the prison camp, when the war was over.

It took a long time to be over. Every day behind that wire fence was like a year.

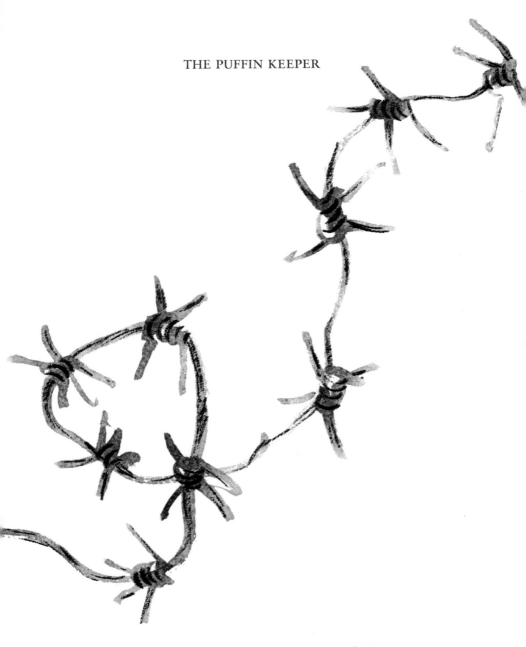

In the end we won, everyone said. I'm not sure wars are ever won.

Chapter Eight

But the world had changed when I got home. I hadn't told Mother I was coming. Someone else answered when I knocked on her cottage door in the village. My mother had moved out a while ago, I was told. She was living down the road in the school now. I was puzzled.

I found her in the vegetable garden. She was picking beans. She seemed pleased to see me, but she looked uncomfortable. She kept looking over my shoulder. "I didn't want to write it in a letter," she began. "I wanted to explain. I'm married again, Allen. I married the art teacher. You remember him, Mr. Carter? Harry? He's a good kind man, and he was very fond of you when you were a boy here. And he loved your pictures. I hope you don't mind, chéri."

It was a strange meeting I had some minutes later in the vegetable garden with Mr. Carter. He didn't seem to know what to say and neither

did I. He made me feel I was about ten years old again, but that wasn't his fault. I told them both that evening where I was going, back to Scilly, that I was thinking of living there and being an artist, which pleased Mr. Carter — I could not think of him as Harry.

"Or I may become a writer," I said, "and you must come and see me one day." It was all very polite, and they were both kind, though Mr. Carter did ask me rather too many questions about my ship being sunk, and how conditions had been in the prisoner of war camp. I didn't want to talk about it. As I looked at them both, I was happy for Mother. The two of them looked right together, contented. This was her adventure, and I had no part in it. I felt more and more during that evening that I was the cuckoo in the nest. So I flew away the next morning, early.

I took the train to Penzance, then the steamer over to Scilly, arriving in late afternoon. It was a glorious crossing, the sea calm and blue about me, gannets diving, porpoises leaping. It felt as if I was sailing into a land of peace, and I promised myself never to leave it again. These islands would be my home.

It was not the same boatman taking me across to Puffin Island. I did not recognize him. "You been over there before, have you? Do you know the Puffin Keeper?"

"The Puffin Keeper?" I said.

"Old Ben. No one calls him Benjamin Postlethwaite no more. He's the Puffin Keeper. You'll soon see why."

Chapter Nine

He was right. The sea all around the island was dotted with floating puffins. And as I came closer I could see them in their hundreds now up at the far end of the island, on the headland above the cliffs, flying in, flying out, but most of them just standing there looking out to sea.

I was coming home, gulls and kittiwakes circling above me, crying out their welcome. The terns and the gannets were still diving, the waves still rolling in. Peace, blessed peace all around me.

Benjamin Postlethwaite met me on the quay. "I been waiting for you," he said. He needed my arm for support as he walked me up to the headland. We stood there with the puffins all around us. "That first one that we mended, you remember him, Allen? He came back and back, then brought his friends with him, and they came to live on the islands, found their old burrows. Then his friends brought their friends. He's still about. I see him limping sometimes.

He knows me, and I know him. He'll know you too, you'll see. Just look at the place, will you? It's Puffin Island again."

He turned to me then, and put his hand on my shoulder. "You staying, or going?"

"Staying," I said.

Chapter Ten

And I did. I stayed with Ben — with our puffin
who did know me — with all the puffins, and a
few years later I brought my wife, Clare, to live
here, in the lighthouse with me, and with Ben
— no longer the lighthouse keeper but a puffin
keeper instead. And our two children have
grown up here too, Millie and John. Mother
and Mr. Carter came to live on St. Mary's when
they retired, to be near us. And that's grand.

We have more visitors on the island these days. But they don't go near the headland where all the puffins live, and neither do we. The Puffin Keeper's Law, we call it. We leave the puffins be.

The visitors buy my pictures, and sometimes the books that I write, and Clare illustrates. She grows vegetables too, the best potatoes in the world, and she keeps bees that make the best heather honey in the world. Often I tell the stories I'm writing to my children. At the moment they like best the one I've just written, called "The Puffin Keeper." The one you've just been reading.

I paint puffins more than ships these days. Ben used to tell me I was a fine artist. He was being kind. Ben was the real artist. You can find Ben's pictures in galleries everywhere, all over

the world. No one paints as he did. He became
quite famous before he died. But, as he said, he
never cared for medals and the like. He wasn't
like that. He always said he lived for his puffins
and his lighthouse, his pictures, and his family.
And we were his family. We are his family.

Afterword

This story is dedicated to Allen Williams Lane. He was the man who founded Penguin Books way back in 1935. He was the real Puffin Man, but also the Pelican Man, and of course the Penguin Man. What a lighthouse he built. And its light still shines all these years later. And the Puffins still fly.

M.M. and C.M.

Michael Morpurgo 11 August 2019

Michael Morpurgo

Michael Morpurgo is one of Britain's best-loved storymakers. He has written over 150 books loved by readers around the world. His best-known work, *War Horse*, was adapted into a film by Steven Spielberg, and also a widely acclaimed play by the National Theatre.

With his wife Clare, Michael has set up the charity *Farms for City Children*. They wanted city children to have the opportunity to live and work on a real farm for a week, and to go home with lifelong memories of the countryside. The charity runs three farms which have welcomed 100,000 children over the last 45 years.

In 2003 Michael became the third Children's Laureate, a position he helped to create with the poet Ted Hughes. In 2017 he was awarded a knighthood for services to literature and charity.

Benji Davies

When he was small, Benji loved stories and he loved to draw. Now he is grown up, he writes and illustrates books for children.

Alongside books illustrated for other authors like this one, he is the creator of several much-loved and bestselling picture books including *The Storm Whale*, *Grandad's Island* and *Tad*, which have all been used by schools to promote visual literacy in the classroom.

His books have won many awards and are read the world over in more than forty languages.

PUFFIN

has been *inspiring* dreams for 80 years.

Since 1940, millions of children have grown up dreaming of snowmen coming to life, rivers of chocolate and Borrowers under the kitchen table. Here's how Puffin's own story began . . .

The first ever Puffin books didn't tell stories, but instead were factual books. In 1940, Allen Lane, the founder of Penguin, published the first four Puffin books aimed at children evacuated to the country because of World War Two — *War on Land* and *War at Sea* by James Holland, and *War in the Air* and *On the Farm* by James Gardner. In that same year, the first female editor for Puffin, Eleanor Graham, set out during an air raid to discuss the launch of a paperback series, Puffin Story Books. In 1941, the first fiction books for children were published, including *Worzel Gummidge* by Barbara Euphan Todd.

In the 1960s Puffin launched the Puffin Club, which at its height had over 200,000 members. The Puffineers even raised money to buy a stretch of the Yorkshire coastline to be used as a puffin sanctuary.

Many Puffin stories have had lives beyond the page, transformed into tales told via film, theater and even computer games. The little bird is recognized around the world and Puffin books have even travelled to outer space, when astronaut Tim Peake read *Goodnight Spaceman* by Michelle Robinson and Nick East from the International Space Station.

Puffin's story is the sum of a million dreams. Some of these dreams are big, and some of them are small. Some are wild, and some are full of love, hope and kindness. There's a dream for everyone and a story for everyone. You just need to decide what you want to dream next . . .